MW01107839

PRO HOCKEY'S CHAMPIONSHIP

BY TYLER OMOTH

CAPSTONE PRESS
a capstone imprint

Blazers Books are published by Capstone Press,
1710 Roe Crest Drive, North Mankato, Minnesota 56003
www.mycapstone.com

Library of Congress Cataloging-in-Publication Data
Names: Omoth, Tyler, author.
Title: Pro hockey's championship / by Tyler Omoth.
Description: North Mankato, Minnesota : An imprint of Capstone Press, [2018]
   | Series: Major Sports Championships | Series: Blazers | Audience: Ages:
   8-14.
Identifiers: LCCN 2017028553 (print) | LCCN 2017032372 (ebook) | ISBN
   9781543504538 (eBook PDF) | ISBN 9781543504934 (hardcover)
Subjects: LCSH: Stanley Cup (Hockey)—History—Juvenile literature. |
   National Hockey League—Juvenile literature. | Hockey—History--Juvenile
   literature.
Classification: LCC GV847.7 (ebook) | LCC GV847.7 .O68 2018 (print) | DDC
   796.962/648—dc23
LC record available at https://lccn.loc.gov/2017028553

Editorial Credits
Carrie Braulick Sheely, editor; Kyle Grenz, designer; Eric Gohl, media researcher;
Kathy McColley, production specialist

Photo Credits
AP Photo: 26; Getty Images: Bruce Bennett, 7, 8, 23, John Iacono, 16–17, 18–19;
Newscom: Icon SMI/Michael Tureski, 13, Icon Sportswire/Robin Alam, 11, Reuters/
Gary Caskey, 25, UPI Photo Service/Gary Wiepert, 28–29, USA Today Sports/Bruce
Bennett, 14–15, USA Today Sports/Dan Hamilton, cover, USA Today Sports/Geoff
Burke, 12, USA Today Sports/Jerry Lai, 5 (top), ZUMA Press/Joel Marklund, 5
(bottom), ZUMA Press/Larry Macdougal, 20

Design Elements: Shutterstock

Printed and bound in the USA.
010754S18

TABLE OF CONTENTS

STANLEY CUP SHOWDOWN

Game 6 of the 2017 Stanley Cup Final was underway. The Nashville Predators were in a showdown with the Pittsburgh Penguins. Both goalies blocked shot after shot. Finally, the Penguins took the lead 1-0. They added a goal to win the title.

FACT The Stanley Cup is named for Lord Stanley of Preston. Stanley bought the original Cup to give to Canada's top **amateur** team.

amateur—describes a sports league that athletes take part in for pleasure rather than for money

Patric Hornqvist sneaks a goal past Predators goalie Pekka Rinne during the 2017 Stanley Cup Final.

Sidney Crosby holds up the Stanley Cup to celebrate the Penguins' 2017 title win.

HISTORY OF THE STANLEY CUP

The Stanley Cup championships are more than 120 years old. At first, the top amateur team in Canada earned the Cup each year. But another team could later **challenge** the winners for it.

challenge—to invite into competition

Montreal won the first Stanley Cup in 1893.

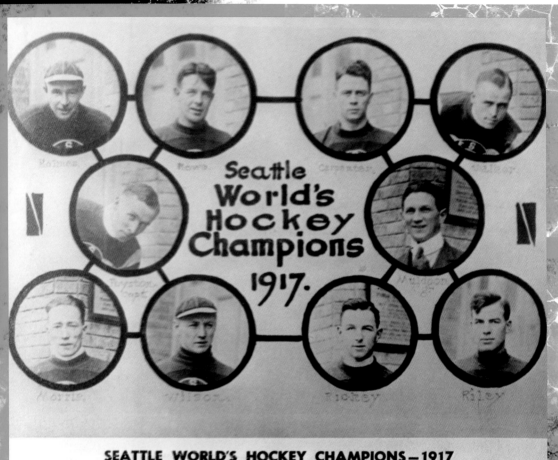

SEATTLE WORLD'S HOCKEY CHAMPIONS – 1917

Back row: left to right—HOLMES   ROWE   CARPENTER   WALKER

Middle row: left to right—FOYSTON   MULDOON

Front row: left to right—MORRIS   WILSON   RICKEY   RILEY

FACT The Montreal Canadiens are the oldest pro hockey team. The team formed in 1909 as part of the NHA.

From 1914 to 1917, the champions of the
Pacific Coast Hockey Association (PCHA) and
the National Hockey Association (NHA) played
for the Stanley Cup. Then the NHA broke apart,
and the National Hockey **League** (NHL) formed.
By 1927 only NHL teams played for the Cup.

MOST TEAM STANLEY CUP WINS

TEAM	WINS
MONTREAL CANADIENS	23
TORONTO MAPLE LEAFS	13
DETROIT RED WINGS	11
BOSTON BRUINS	6
CHICAGO BLACKHAWKS	6

league—a group of sports teams

THE *ROAD* TO THE STANLEY CUP

Today 30 NHL teams start each season. Teams play 82 games during the regular season. They get two points for each win. They receive zero points for a loss in regular time. They earn one point for a loss in **overtime** or a **shootout**.

overtime—an extra period played if the score is tied at the end of a game

shootout—a method of breaking a tie score at the end of an overtime period

The Tampa Bay Lightning and the Chicago Blackhawks face off for the Cup in 2015. In Game 6 the Blackhawks won, claiming their third title in six seasons.

The Washington Capitals battle it out against the
Toronto Maple Leafs in a 2017 playoff game.

The teams are split into two conferences. The top eight teams in each conference reach the playoffs. Teams play three rounds of playoffs to decide the conference winners.

After each playoff series, it is a tradition for the two teams to shake hands.

The conference champions face off in the Stanley Cup Final series. The Stanley Cup Final is a best-of-seven series. The first team to win four games is the NHL champion.

Pittsburgh Penguins goalie Matt Murray makes a save against San Jose Shark Joonas Donskoi in the 2016 Stanley Cup Final.

GREATEST DYNASTIES

Some teams win enough to be called **dynasties**. The Montreal Canadiens won 18 Stanley Cup titles from 1944 to 1979. During this time, they reached the finals 24 times.

Montreal Canadiens players Serge Savard (left) and Yvan Cournoyer hold the Stanley Cup after winning the title in 1978.

dynasty—a team that wins multiple championships over a period of several years

17

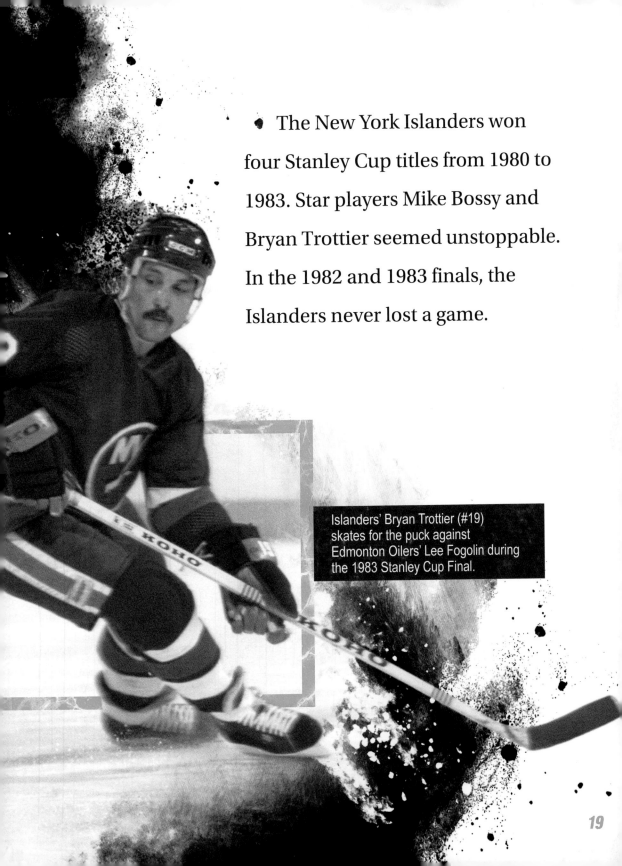

The New York Islanders won four Stanley Cup titles from 1980 to 1983. Star players Mike Bossy and Bryan Trottier seemed unstoppable. In the 1982 and 1983 finals, the Islanders never lost a game.

Islanders' Bryan Trottier (#19) skates for the puck against Edmonton Oilers' Lee Fogolin during the 1983 Stanley Cup Final.

In 1984 a different NHL team rose to dynasty fame. The Edmonton Oilers scored easily and often. Superstar Wayne Gretzky led the team to win after win. The Oilers won five Stanley Cup titles from 1984 to 1990.

Edmonton Oilers' Dave Semenko celebrates a goal during a 1984 game.

MEMORABLE MOMENTS

Many moments stand out in Stanley Cup history. Among them are the 1988 finals between the Oilers and the Boston Bruins. Wayne Gretzky was on fire. He scored a whopping 13 points in the Oilers' four-game **sweep**.

Wayne Gretzky (front) skates near defender Steve Kasper during the 1988 Stanley Cup Final.

sweep—when a team wins a series without losing to the opposing team

MOST POINTS SCORED IN A STANLEY CUP FINAL SERIES

NAME	TEAM	YEAR	POINTS
WAYNE GRETZKY	EDMONTON	1988	13
GORDIE HOWE	DETROIT	1955	12
YVAN COURNOYER	MONTREAL	1973	12
JACQUES LEMAIRE	MONTREAL	1973	12
MARIO LEMIEUX	PITTSBURGH	1991	12

In 2001 the New Jersey Devils won three of the first five games in the finals. But then Colorado Avalanche goalie Patrick Roy worked his magic. He allowed only one goal in the last two games. The Avalanche won the Cup.

Patrick Roy stops a shot on goal in the 2001 Stanley Cup Final.

GOALTENDER CAREER PLAYOFF SHUTOUTS

GOALTENDER	SHUTOUTS
MARTIN BRODEUR	24
PATRICK ROY	23
CURTIS JOSEPH	16
CHRIS OSGOOD	15

shutout—when the opposing team doesn't score

FACT The 1942 finals series was the first to go
to seven games in Stanley Cup history.

In 1942 the Toronto Maple Leafs lost the first three games of the finals to the Detroit Red Wings. With **rookies** playing, the Maple Leafs squeaked out the Game 4 win. They went on to win the next three games! No team has won the Cup from a 0-3 finals record since.

Maple Leafs captain Syl Apps accepts the Stanley Cup from NHL President Frank Calder in 1942.

rookie—a first-year player

In Game 6 of the 1999 finals, Dallas Stars' Brett Hull shot the puck into the net. People said it broke the rules because Hull's foot was in the **crease**. But the goal counted. The Stars beat the Buffalo Sabres and took home the Cup.

crease—the area directly in front of the goal; the crease is often painted blue

Sabres fans refer to Hull's shot as the "No Goal." The NHL changed its rule about a player's foot being in the crease the next year.

Sabres goalie Dominik Hasek pinned the puck against Hull's stick just before Hull shot the game-winning goal.

Glossary

amateur (AM-uh-chur)—describes a sports league that athletes take part in for pleasure rather than for money

challenge (CHAL-uhnj)—to invite into competition

crease (KREES)—the area directly in front of the goal; the crease is often painted blue

dynasty (DYE-nuh-stee)—a team that wins multiple championships over a period of several years

league (LEEG)—a group of sports teams

overtime (OH-vur-time)—an extra period played if the score is tied at the end of a game

rookie (RUK-ee)—a first-year player

shootout (SHOOT-out)—a method of breaking a tie score at the end of an overtime period

shutout (SHUHT-out)—when the opposing team doesn't score

sweep (SWEEP)—when a team wins a series without losing to the opposing team

tradition (truh-DISH-uhn)—a custom, idea, or belief passed down through time

Read More

Doeden, Matt. *All About Hockey.* All About Sports. North Mankato, Minn.: Capstone, 2015.

Nagelhout, Ryan. *Sidney Crosby.* Sports MVPs. New York: Gareth Stevens, 2016.

Storden, Thom. *Amazing Hockey Records.* Epic Sports Records. North Mankato, Minn.: Capstone, 2015.

Winters, Jaime. *Center Ice: The Stanley Cup.* Hockey Source. New York: Crabtree, 2015.

Internet Sites

Use FactHound to find Internet sites related to this book.

Visit *www.facthound.com*

Just type in **9781543504934** and go.

Super-cool stuff! Check out projects, games and lots more at **www.capstonekids.com**

Index